The Riddle of Dr Sphinx

The Riddle of Dr Sphinx

Margaret Ryan
Illustrated by Kate Pankhurst

A & C Black • London

For Andrew and Granny Elspeth with love

First published 2009 by
A & C Black Publishers Ltd
36 Soho Square, London, W1D 3QY

www.acblack.com

Text copyright © 2009 Margaret Ryan
Illustrations copyright © 2009 Kate Pankhurst

ISBN 978-1-4081-0493-4

A CIP catalogue for this book is available from the British Library.

Printed and bound in Great Britain
by CPI Cox & Wyman, Reading, RG1 8EX.

The problem: My old bike. I am growing too big for it, but we can't afford a new one as Dad is off work with a broken leg.

The brainwave: Ask Mr Maini at the corner shop if he has a paper round so I can save up for some new wheels.

The dilemma: There is a paper round, but it takes in Weir Street and I've heard that the people who live there are weird.

The hero: Me, of course. Jonny Smith. I'm not scared – it's only a paper round. And just how weird can the people in Weir Street be...?

Chapter One

It was Monday morning and I was cycling to Mr Maini's shop to collect the papers for my round. I have to get up early to be there on time, and I find it really hard. But Mr Maini's always smiling and cheerful.

Not today.

"Ah, there you are, Jonny," he said. "I'm afraid I've received a complaint about you from one of my customers."

A complaint? I thought hard. What had I done?

"Er, some of the Weir Street numbers are a bit strange," I said. "Did someone get the wrong paper?"

"No," said Mr Maini. "But there is someone who has to look in his garden for the paper every morning because it doesn't get delivered to his house."

"Oh," I said. "That'll be Dr Sphinx, the archaeologist, at number 36."

Mr Maini nodded. "He doesn't mind in dry weather, but when it's raining his paper is a soggy mess."

"Sorry," I said. "I hadn't thought of that. But don't worry, I'll take it right up to the front door today… If I can find it," I added under my breath.

"Good," smiled Mr Maini, and handed me my big orange bag.

But it *wasn't* good.

The truth is, I have never actually seen Dr Sphinx's house. Never even got *close* to it. As soon as I open the creaky gate, I start to feel shaky. The garden is so overgrown it's like entering a jungle. Tall grasses brush my ears, and spiky plants tug at my clothes. Enormous spiders swing past and leave webs that cling to my face and hair. I brush them away immediately, but I'm sure I can feel millions of spiderlings scuttle down my neck.

Then there are the strange rustlings. Sounds that say something scary is lurking in the undergrowth, just out of sight, ready to pounce... That's why I always throw the paper in the direction of the house, and get out of there ... fast.

But now Dr Sphinx has complained, so that won't do. Now I will have to open the creaky gate and wade my way through the shoulder-high grass. Now I will have to do my best to ignore the strange rustling sounds and the spiders' webs. Now I will have to try to find the front door of number 36, deliver the paper, and somehow get back out of there alive…

I slung the orange bag over my shoulder, jumped on my bike and headed for Weird Street. I stopped at number 13 to deliver Captain Cross-eyed's paper. Scarface Jack, his one-eared cat, was sitting on the doorstep, but the huge pirate was nowhere to be seen.

I delivered a few more papers before I got to number 34 and a half. Mr Tipp the inventor and his robots live there. His house is built right into the side of the hill and has an oak door that used to belong to a castle. There's no letter box, so I always leave the paper in the old milk churn on the step. Today, I didn't see Mr Tipp or any of his robots, but I *did* hear a muffled explosion coming from inside the house.

"Mr Tipp's busy inventing again," I smiled.

Then I stopped smiling. The next house was number 36. The house belonging to Dr Sphinx. The house I had never actually seen. I plucked up my courage and opened the gate. In front of me, the shoulder-high grass moved gently in the breeze. And I could hear rustling sounds. I parted the grass and started to go forwards. The rustling sounds got closer. And closer...

Suddenly, I was aware of eyes watching me. Of ears listening to me. Of whiskers twitching at me.

Suddenly, I was surrounded by cats. Cats of all colours. Some dark, some light, some patchy, some stripy. They came in all sizes, too, and there was one that had an artificial leg with a tiny wheel on the end. Her name was Inca. I'd met her before, and I knew that Mr Tipp had made the leg after she'd lost her real one in a car accident. But the cats had one thing in common – they were all gazing at me unblinkingly. Except for a big orange one. He arched his back and gave a bad tempered *HISSSSS*.

I hissed right back. "I've got a cat called Noggin and I'm not scared of you," I said. I hoped I sounded braver than I felt.

I crept forwards, with the cats slinking along at my heels, until I came upon a pyramid-shaped wooden box. A startled cat leapt out of it.

MIAOW!

"Sorry, Tiger," I gasped. I'd met him before, too, and recognised him by his stripy tail.

Tiger gave me a green-eyed stare, then scampered off through the long grass. Perhaps he knows where the house is, I thought, and followed him as best I could.

Soon I came to a clearing, and there at last was the house. At least, I *think* it was a house, but it wasn't like our terraced one. It looked more like a ruined temple, with a grand entrance and tall columns on either side of the front door. The door had an old-fashioned car horn nailed to it. Above the horn was a notice saying TOOT AND COME IN.

"No way," I muttered, and looked for a letter box.

But there wasn't one.

"Oh well," I shrugged. A lot of the houses in Weird Street had no letter boxes. I was just about to put the paper into what looked like a big, stone horse trough, when a loud gong sounded.

BONNNNNG!

I got such a fright I stepped back and fell into the trough. The orange cat leapt onto the edge and hissed at me so loudly I thought he was going to pounce.

"Help! Help!" I yelled, and my voice echoed back.

Chapter Two

I was still struggling to get out of the trough, when Dr Sphinx appeared. He wore an old pith helmet and a faded shirt and shorts. He picked up the orange cat and placed him on the ground.

"Go into the house, Diogenes," he said. Then he looked at me. "You're the paperboy. I'm glad you've found your way to the house at last. But, tell me, what are you doing in my sarcophagus?"

"Sarcopha– what?"

"Stone coffin," said Dr Sphinx.

YIKES!

I clambered out quickly, scraping my knees on the side.

"I didn't mean… I mean, I didn't know…
I mean…"

Dr Sphinx looked down his nose at me.
"You didn't know it was a coffin? You mean,
you couldn't read the writing on the side?"

Writing? I bent down and looked more
closely. There were some vertical marks
on the side of the sarcophagus, but they
looked more like little pictures to me.
I thought I could make out an arm and a
few small birds.

"It's very different to the writing we do in school," I said.

Dr Sphinx nodded. "I would be happy to explain it to you, but I've already sounded the gong for the cats' breakfast, so I must go and feed them. Come another time if you want to discover the riddle of the writing."

"I will," I said. "I'd like that." I wanted to know more about the writing *and* about Dr Sphinx and his odd house. Perhaps there were some even stranger things inside...

I made my way back through the long grass and jumped onto my bike. Then I pedalled to school as fast as I could. When I got there, the playground was empty, apart from a crow pecking at some cold chips someone had thrown away.

"Oh no, late again," I groaned.

I hurried along to my classroom. Miss Dodds was busy at the whiteboard, but she heard me tiptoe in. She frowned. Then she saw my scraped knees. "Oh dear, that looks painful, Jonny. Did you fall off your bike? Is that why you're late?"

$57 \div 6 =$
$106 \times 27 =$
maths quiz

Now it would have been sensible just to say "yes". But my dad says it's important to always tell the truth, so I did.

"No, I got a fright when a loud gong sounded at Dr Sphinx's house, which looks like a ruined temple, and I fell into a stone coffin with funny writing on the side, and I scraped my knees getting out."

The class gasped and my friends, Sara and Surinder, sighed and shook their heads.

Miss Dodds breathed in deeply through her long nose. "When are you going to start being sensible, Jonny Smith," she said, "and stop telling these silly stories?"

I just shrugged and looked at my knees. While I was doing my paper round in Weird Street, I didn't think it would be any time soon.

At least Sara and Surinder believed me.

"Dr Sphinx sounds a bit spooky," said Sara, at break.

"Maybe we should come with you to see the stone coffin," said Surinder.

"Sarcophagus, you mean," said Sara, who can be a bit of a brainbox sometimes, and is really keen on history.

"I don't suppose Dr Sphinx would mind," I said.

"Saturday, then. After your round," said Sara.

"No, I have to go straight home on Saturday to get ready for the inter-schools' football final."

"And I've got to visit my aunt on Sunday," said Surinder.

"Weekdays are out," I said. "I'm helping Dad in the garden after school to earn money for my new bike fund. It'll have to be the following Saturday."

"But that's ages away," said Sara.

"Sorry," I said, and glanced at my knees. "Now, I'd better clean these up before I go to see Mr McGregor."

Mr McGregor's our football coach. He really wants us to win the inter-schools' championship, but he's been a bit grumpy recently. He must be worried about the match.

"What have you done to your knees, Smith?" he demanded at football practice. "Did you fall off that wee bike of yours?"

"No," I shook my head. "I tripped over."

"Well, learn to look where you're going," he said. "I hope you can still run, otherwise I'll drop you from the team."

I gritted my teeth and ran out onto the playing field. My knees *did* hurt, but I was determined to keep my place for the final.

Chapter Three

When I got home, I told Mum all about Dr Sphinx.

"I've met him," she said. "He came to our mothers' group to give a talk on ancient Egypt. He's a very interesting man."

"Talking about me?" asked Dad, hobbling in from the garden on his crutches. Dad's a community policeman, but he broke his leg while chasing some thieves, so he's at home most of the time right now.

"No," I smiled, and told him the story about Dr Sphinx, too.

"So *that's* what's behind all the grass at number 36," he said. "Mind you, if Jonny and I don't get the mower out soon, ours will be just as high. Maybe we should get a goat."

"Haven't we got enough animals with a dog, a goldfish and a cat," sighed Mum.

❧

That night, I had a strange dream. In it, I was surrounded by orange cats who started hissing, then chasing me. I raced away as fast as I could, but my legs felt very heavy and slow.

After a while, some of the cats caught up with me and ran under my feet. I tried to jump over them but I couldn't. Instead, I got tangled up and could feel myself falling, falling, falling ... right out of bed. *Thump*!

I picked myself up, rubbed the sleep from my eyes, and looked at the clock. It was still early, and I really *did* want to know more about that funny writing. If I set off now...

I grabbed a cereal bar and jumped on my bike. I delivered my papers as usual, but left Dr Sphinx's house till last.

At number 36, I parked my bike and slowly opened the creaky gate. I still felt a bit shaky, but I took a deep breath to steady myself, and headed into the long grass. An early-morning mist hung in the air giving everything a ghostly look, and I shivered as the wet grass trailed across my clothes.

Then something brushed my leg. I let out a yell. But it was only Tiger.

Dr Sphinx must have heard me shout, because he came out of his strange house to meet me.

"Jonny Smith," he smiled. "You're here early today."

"I wanted to find out the riddle of the writing on the sarcophagus."

"Of course," said Dr Sphinx. "Come with me." He walked over to the stone coffin, and I knelt down beside him while he explained what the odd marks meant.

"This is ancient Egyptian writing," he said. "The ancient Egyptians wrote from top to bottom, and in pictures. If you look carefully, you can see three reed leaves, two quail chicks, an arm, water, a mouth, an owl, a chick and two leaves, another owl, a chick, two more owls, a chick and two leaves."

"I see that now," I said excitedly. "But what does it mean?"

Dr Sphinx grinned. "It means the person who made this sarcophagus was a real joker. These pictures say I WANT MY MUMMY."

I gasped.

"Would you like to meet *my* mummy?" asked Dr Sphinx.

"Sure. You met mine at the mothers' group."

"But yours isn't an ancient Egyptian, or three thousand years old."

"Not quite," I grinned and checked my watch. "But I'll be late for school if I don't leave now. Can I see it tomorrow?"

"Certainly."

I thanked Dr Sphinx and headed back to my bike. I was hurtling down Weird Street when a cat darted out in front of me. I braked hard and stopped so suddenly I fell off my bike.

"Oh no, my poor knees," I moaned, and dragged myself and my bike onto the pavement.

The cat watched me from a safe distance.

"Inca!" I gasped. "You shouldn't be out here. I'd better take you home."

I picked her up and limped back up the hill to number 36, where I dropped her in the long grass.

"Now, stay there," I said. "Or you're going to lose another leg."

She disappeared without looking back. Then I collected my bike and pedalled slowly to school.

When I arrived, the playground was empty.

Miss Dodds gave me one of her fiercest looks when I entered the classroom.

"Well, what's this morning's fantastic excuse for being late?" she asked.

"I fell off my bike when a three-legged cat that had an artificial leg with a wheel on the end ran out in front of me," I said.

"Silly boy," said Miss Dodds. But I didn't get off that lightly. "Stay behind at break. I want a word with you."

Actually, Miss Dodds wanted *several* words. Words like "no more football practice if you're late for school again".

"But it's the inter-schools' final on Saturday, and I'm in the team," I gasped.

"I'm aware of that," said Miss Dodds. "So, it's up to you, Jonny. The choice is yours."

Chapter Four

"I can't be late for school again," I muttered to Sara and Surinder. "If I am, Miss Dodds will ban me from football practice and Mr McGregor'll kill me. But I really did want to see that mummy, especially after hearing the joke on the sarcophagus…"

Sara and Surinder looked at each other. "What mummy? What joke?"

I told them.

Sara was thoughtful. "Perhaps we could help you with your paper round tomorrow," she said. "Then we could come and see the mummy, too."

"And the sarcophagus with the joke on it," said Surinder.

"The end of next week's too long to wait," they both agreed.

"OK," I grinned. "Meet me at Mr Maini's at seven o'clock."

"That's early!" gasped Surinder.

But they were both there on time, yawning and leaning on their bikes.

"I see you have friends with you today, Jonny," said Mr Maini.

"They've come to help," I said.

Mr Maini handed me the papers and I divided them up into three bundles.

"You've got Captain Cross-eyed's paper. You might see Scarface Jack," I told Sara.

"And you've got Miss King's paper, Surinder. You'll see a fierce-looking, stone Viking warrior at her house."

"Can't wait," they grinned, and pedalled away.

"Meet me outside number 36 when you're finished," I called.

I set off, too. My bag was much lighter than usual and I got through my bit of the round quickly, finishing off with Mr Tipp at number 34 and a half. In no time, Sara and Surinder and I were all standing on the pavement outside the gate of number 36.

"Right," I said, feeling braver with my friends beside me. "Here we go." I opened the gate and plunged into the shoulder-high grass.

"You were right. It *is* like a jungle in here," muttered Surinder, keeping close behind me.

"Something just brushed past my leg," squeaked Sara.

"That'll be Tiger," I said. We followed in single file until the house came into view.

"Wow," breathed Sara. "It *does* look like an old temple."

"I can see the funny writing on the sarcophagus," muttered Surinder, stooping down to peer at the pictures.

"But I don't see Dr Sphinx," I said. "I wonder where he is."

As if he'd understood what I was saying, Tiger blinked at me and headed for the door of the house.

I paused. "What should we do?"

"Well, it says toot and come in," said Sara.

I squeezed the bulb of the horn. *TOOT!*

At the sudden noise, Inca and Diogenes and their friends appeared. Diogenes came towards us, arching his orange back and hissing.

"Perhaps we'd better go inside," I said.

We entered the house and found ourselves in a dark, narrow passageway whose walls were cold and rough to the touch.

"This is scary," whispered Sara.

"But exciting," breathed Surinder.

35

I said nothing. Where was Dr Sphinx? Perhaps we should go back. But the cats, including the angry Diogenes, were right behind us.

At that moment, the passageway opened out into a large room. Sunlight filtered through the narrow windows showing the strange hieroglyphics covering the walls. Broken jars, some with lids

with animal heads covered the tables, and bits of old stone littered the floor. There was dust everywhere. Dust and paw prints.

"It's not like a proper house," I said. "There's hardly any furniture. Just a lot of ... rubbish."

"Ancient objects, you mean," said a familiar voice, and Dr Sphinx appeared from a hidden door in the far wall.

"Oh, er, hello," I said. "Sorry, I mean…
We did knock, er toot…"

"You are welcome." Dr Sphinx stooped
to pick up Diogenes, who was still hissing.
"Behave," he told the cat. "These children
won't hurt you. They are Jonny's friends."

"Sara and Surinder," I said.

"I'm very interested in ancient things,"
said Sara.

"And I've never seen a real mummy
before," said Surinder.

"Then prepare to be amazed," smiled
Dr Sphinx, and led us to a tall cupboard
in a dark corner. He felt in the pocket of
his shirt, took out a large key, and unlocked
the cupboard door. It creaked open. The
three of us shivered with excitement.

Inside the cupboard was a tall, glass
case. We leaned forwards to peer at it. And
there, staring back at us, all bandaged up,
was an ancient Egyptian mummy.

Chapter Five

"I'd like you to meet Fred," said Dr Sphinx, smiling.

"A mummy called Fred!" we exclaimed.

"My little joke," smiled Dr Sphinx. "I can find no record of his Egyptian name. He was in one of the lesser tombs I helped to uncover. Unfortunately, he wasn't in very good condition and nobody seemed to want him, so I brought him home with me."

"Have you got all of him?" asked Sara.

All of him? What was she on about?

"His intestines, you mean?" Dr Sphinx said. "No. Many things were destroyed by tomb robbers, but his liver or lungs might still be in a jar somewhere, who knows?"

Liver? Lungs? I looked at the old jars lying around.

"Don't worry. These ones are all empty," smiled Dr Sphinx. "Just like Fred's head."

"The brains are sliced up by sticking a hook up the nose," nodded Sara. "Then the skull is washed out. I read all about it."

I told you she liked history.

Surinder was really interested in the cats, who were now sitting completely still, apart from Diogenes. He had jumped out of Dr Sphinx's arms and was pacing around.

"Why have you got so many cats?" he asked. "And why is Dio – that orange one – so restless?"

"Cats were considered gods in ancient Egypt, so they're very important. And I like cats. But Diogenes, that's the name I gave him, arrived here very recently. Someone just threw him into the long grass outside my house. Perhaps they didn't want him, I don't know. But it's made him very frightened and upset. He's a bit of a problem. Actually, they all are. I have to go back to Egypt unexpectedly. A new tomb has been discovered and my help is needed..."

And, as if they knew they were being talked about, the cats formed a circle round

Dr Sphinx. He stooped to tickle their ears, then they came over to us and let us stroke them, too. Inca even licked my hand. Only Diogenes stayed well away, still pacing, still fretful.

Then I noticed the time. "I'm sorry… We must go now, Dr Sphinx, or we'll be late for school. Thank you for showing us your mummy."

"Come again," said Dr Sphinx and waved us off.

"See you at school," I called to Sara and Surinder, as we pedalled away.

∽◯∽

For the next two days it rained. Not just a light drizzle, but a skull-drumming downpour.

Sara and Surinder didn't come with me on my round. They hadn't enjoyed getting up early and had come up with another plan to help me get to school on time.

Head down, I pedalled through the rain, trying to make sure the papers stayed dry. Which was more than I was. Raindrops trickled down my neck, slid under my collar, then raced each other down my back.

I must be mad doing this, I thought, wiping my eyes.

But at least Dr Sphinx's cats were being sensible. At number 36, I found some of them sheltering in the pyramid-shaped boxes, while others were tucked up inside the sarcophagus. They miaowed a greeting when I popped the paper in beside them, though Diogenes jumped up onto the edge and hissed, as usual.

"Shush," I told him. "I'm your friend, remember. And you'll need some of those when Dr Sphinx goes back to Egypt. You can't be left to look after yourselves."

I was still thinking about this when I handed my bag back to Mr Maini. As I was leaving the shop, I spotted something in the window. Something which gave me a brilliant idea. Sometimes I think I might be a genius. I often get brilliant ideas. But I had no time to do anything about it then.

I headed for school, hung my dripping jacket in the cloakroom, and just managed to nip through the classroom door ahead of Miss Dodds. Thanks to Sara. She had stopped her in the corridor to ask all sorts of questions about ancient Egypt.

"I'll stop Miss Dodds tomorrow, if you're late," whispered Surinder, as I sat down. "I'll bring in all my family's Diwali photos to show her. There are hundreds of them."

Being asked intelligent questions by Sara had put Miss Dodds in a good mood. But someone was *not*. At football practice, Mr McGregor was grumpier than ever.

"What are you using for brains today, Smith?" he yelled. "Keep your eye on the ball."

I did my best, but it wasn't easy. Rain dripped off my hair into my eyes, and I slipped and slid all over the pitch. So did everyone else. It was a complete mud bath and, in the end, we had to abandon play.

"Let's just hope the other team play as badly as you lot on Saturday," Mr McGregor muttered, as we trooped inside to get cleaned up. "I wish this rain would stop."

But it didn't.

It rained all night long and, at assembly next morning, it was announced that there would be no football practice. Worse still, at the end of the day, Mr McGregor came into the classroom with a face as thundery as the weather. "The inter-schools' final has been cancelled," he said. "Or at least postponed for a week."

"Oh no!" I whispered to Surinder. "That means a whole extra week that I have to be on time for school."

Then I remembered my brilliant idea. As I didn't have to play football, at least I would have more time to work on that.

Chapter Six

What I had noticed in Mr Maini's shop window was a row of postcards. Some offered things for sale, like washing machines or prams. Some offered services, like window cleaning or gardening. But the one which had caught my eye said:

BOA CONSTRICTOR NEEDS GOOD HOME. OWNER GOING TO ANTARCTICA.

call 01748544

Bit chilly for a snake, I thought. And that's when the idea had come to me. Maybe Dr Sphinx could find good homes for his cats while *he* was away.

When I delivered his paper the next morning, I mentioned it to him.

"That's a great idea, Jonny," he said. "Last time I had to go to Egypt, I put the cats in a cattery, but it made them very unhappy and they went off their food."

"I'll ask the people on my round if they'll help, and my dad knows a lot of people he can ask, too."

"Inca needs special care," said Dr Sphinx. "And Diogenes will certainly be a problem."

"I've got someone in mind for Inca," I smiled, and went next door to deliver the paper to Mr Tipp.

I found him in his garden shed, in the middle of all the junk he uses for his inventions.

"You're early this morning, Jonny," he smiled. "Is Miss Dodds cross with you again?"

"Yes, but that's not why." And I told him about Dr Sphinx's problem with the cats.

"I just wondered," I went on, "if you could look after Inca while he's away. You would be able to fix her leg if the wheel came off."

"Of course," said Mr Tipp. "Inca and I are old friends."

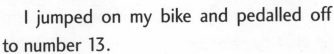

"Thanks, Mr Tipp," I smiled. That was *one* cat sorted out.

I jumped on my bike and pedalled off to number 13.

Captain Cross-eyed opened his door as I went down the path.

"Up with the lark this morning, Jonny," he smiled. "Is Miss Dodds on the warpath again?"

Funny how everyone knew about Miss Dodds!

"Yes, but that's not why I'm early," I said, and repeated my story. "I know Tiger's your favourite," I added, "and I just wondered if you could look after him for a while."

"So long as he doesn't disturb Scarface Jack when he's snoozing, I think it would be all right," smiled Captain Cross-eyed. "Tiger roams a lot anyway."

"Great," I said. My idea was working.

I managed to find homes for two more cats with Ursula Bend, the acrobat, who lived at number 19.

"I just love the way they move," she smiled. "And Dr Sphinx's cats often come and watch me exercising." Then she curled herself up into a ball, just like a cat.

William Izzard at number 21 also said he would help. "The little black cat's often in my garden," he admitted.

Then Mr and Mrs Woyka at number 23 agreed to look after one, too. "It can sit on my knee and keep me company while I'm listening to my music," smiled Mrs Woyka. "Mr Woyka is always so busy with his clocks."

I delivered the rest of my papers and scooted off to school. I only just made it in time. As I passed Surinder in the corridor showing Miss Dodds the last of his Diwali photographs, I gave him a wink.

But Miss Dodds saw the wink and was suspicious.

"I hope you don't think you can be late for school just because the football pitch is waterlogged, Jonny Smith," she said.

"Oh no," I said wide-eyed, and hurried into the classroom.

I told Sara what I'd been doing. "I'd love to help, Jonny," she said, "but my little brother's allergic to cat hair."

"I'm allergic to my sister," grinned Surinder, sitting down behind me, "but I'll ask my mum if we can have one."

I asked my mum, too, after school, but she shook her head. "Brutus is used to cats, but another cat would upset Noggin, as well as the goldfish," she said.

I knew she was right, but I was a bit disappointed, till my gran came to tea.

"I'd be happy to take one," she said. "Cats are good company and don't need to be walked like a dog."

Then Dad said he would have a word with his friend, who works at the local care home. "The old people love it when folks bring their pets in for a visit. I'm sure they'd enjoy looking after a cat for a while."

Even Mr Maini, when I asked him to put up the postcard asking for good homes for the cats, offered to look after one.

"I have heard some scrabblings in the night that might be mice," he said. "A cat could be useful."

Things were turning out even better than I'd hoped, but there were still two more cats who needed homes. Then Mum persuaded the lady who ran the toddlers' group to have one, which only left Diogenes. Now who could I find to look after him?

As I got into class next day, just before Miss Dodds, a thought struck me.

"I don't suppose *you* like cats, Miss Dodds?"

"Horrible smelly creatures," she sniffed.

I should have guessed. I'd just have to find someone else who did.

Chapter Seven

The next day was Saturday. The day I *should* have been playing in the inter-schools' final. But, instead of dodging the opposing team, I was walking our dog and dodging the puddles. I was also wracking my brains trying to think of someone who might look after a problem cat.

"Trouble is, it needs to be someone who understands them," I told Brutus. "Diogenes is definitely difficult."

"Talking to yourself, laddie?" said a familiar voice behind me.

I turned round. It was Mr McGregor, dressed in running vest and shorts.

"Er, I was just telling Brutus about a problem cat that needs a home for a while," I said.

"Oh?" He slowed to walk beside me. "Who's that then?"

I told him the story.

Mr McGregor looked thoughtful. "Maybe I could help you out. I love cats, but Diogenes might not like me. I'd have to meet him first."

"If you've got time, we could go to Weir Street and see Dr Sphinx and Diogenes right now."

"OK," said Mr McGregor. "I can finish my run later."

He took Brutus's lead. "Come on, boy," he said. "Lift up those paws."

Mr McGregor set off at a cracking pace, and by the time we reached number 36, I was puffed out. "It's good training for next week," he laughed.

I blew out my cheeks, opened the gate, and plunged into the shoulder-high grass. "It's this way."

We hadn't got very far when Tiger appeared. As soon as he saw Brutus, Tiger turned tail and fled, and we continued on our way towards the house.

As usual, most of the cats were sheltering inside the sarcophagus, but there was no sign of Diogenes.

"Perhaps he's inside with Dr Sphinx," I said, and tooted the horn.

Dr Sphinx opened the door.

"Hello, Dr Sphinx," I said. "This is my football coach, Mr McGregor. He might be able to look after Diogenes for you while you're away."

"But only if he likes me," said Mr McGregor.

"Of course. Come in and meet him," said Dr Sphinx.

He led the way down the long, narrow passageway and into the big room with the rubbish – sorry, ancient objects. The light was dim, and at first I couldn't see Diogenes anywhere. Then I glimpsed the flick of an ear and a flash of green eyes from behind one of the bigger jars. The eyes blinked once then ... ZIP ... an orange streak launched itself through the air and landed on Mr McGregor's chest.

Mr McGregor staggered back, clutching Diogenes.

"Oh, I'm so sorry," gasped Dr Sphinx, and rushed to remove him.

But there was no need. Mr McGregor wasn't upset. In fact, he was grinning from ear to ear. And Diogenes wasn't upset, either. He was purring fit to burst.

"This isn't Diogenes," laughed Mr McGregor. "This is Donald. And he's not your cat, he's mine!"

What?

"I was taking Donald to the vet," explained Mr McGregor, "and had put his basket on the pavement while I sorted out a parking ticket, when some youths roared past on a motorbike and scooped him up. I got back into the car and gave chase, but they disappeared down an alleyway. I've been looking for him ever since." He stroked the cat's ginger head.

"He's clearly yours," smiled Dr Sphinx. "I've never seen him so happy."

"And I'll be happy to have him home," said Mr McGregor.

"Now I have good homes for all of my cats. Thanks to Jonny," said Dr Sphinx.

"Aye, he's not a bad wee laddie." Mr McGregor smiled at me, then, tucking Donald under his arm, he went off whistling.

I was about to leave with Brutus, but Dr Sphinx told me to stay.

"I have something for you, Jonny," he said. "Something to say thank you for all your help in finding homes for my cats." And he handed me a small, curiously shaped bit of pottery with a blue insect painted on it. "It's an ancient Egyptian charm. Keep it in your pocket and it'll bring you good luck."

"Thank you," I said. "Perhaps it'll help me get to school on time in the morning."

But it didn't. The following Monday, Miss King at number 57 kept me waiting for ages while she went to fetch a list of magazines she wanted to order from Mr Maini. So I was late again.

"You've been warned countless times about being late, Jonny Smith. You will go and tell Mr McGregor you are banned from football practice," said Miss Dodds.

Oh no, I thought. There goes my place in the team *and* the final.

I sighed deeply and headed for the gym. I knew Mr McGregor would be angry.

But he wasn't. "Leave it with me, laddie," he said. "I'll have a word with Miss Dodds."

And he did. I don't know *exactly* what he said, but I think he must have still been really pleased to get Donald back, because I got to go to football practice after all. I had to do a punishment exercise at break instead, though.

"So much for the good-luck charm," I muttered to Sara and Surinder. "It obviously doesn't work." I took it out of my pocket and laid it on the desk.

"This is a scarab-beetle amulet," said Sara, picking it up. "The ancient Egyptians carried one with them at all times. I love things like that. If you don't want it, I'll buy it from you."

"OK," I grinned. "I can put the cash towards my new bike."

Sara came round after school with the money and I popped it into the metal box where I keep my bike fund.

I was just sliding the box back into its hiding place underneath my smelly sock pile when a thought struck me. Dr Sphinx had been right. I just hadn't realised it. The ancient Egyptian amulet *had* brought me luck, after all.

My new bike fund was growing nicely and soon I'd be able to buy the wheels I had my eye on. Unless, that is, something strange happened to make me lose my paper round. And, in Weird Street, how likely was that?